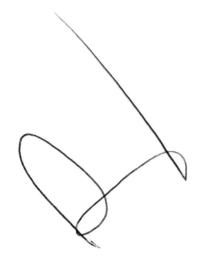

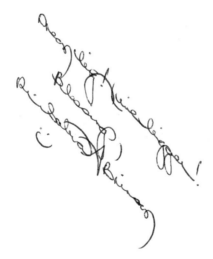

Meet the Philadelphia Dolly Vardens

Inspired by the first African American
women's professional baseball team

by

Dr. Sabrina A. Brinson

tpg

© 2020 Dr. Sabrina A. Brinson
All Rights Reserved

Published by Treehouse Publishing Group
an imprint of Amphorae Publishing Group
4168 Hartford Street, Saint Louis, MO 63116
a woman- and veteran-owned business
www.amphoraepublishing.com

ISBN: 9781732139176
Library of Congress Control Number:

PUBLISHER'S NOTE
Without limiting the rights under the copyright reserved above, no part of this publication may be reproduced, stored in or introduced into a retrieval system, or transmitted, in any form or by any means (electronic, mechanical, photocopying, recording or otherwise), without the prior written permission of both the copyright owner and the above publisher of this book.

Manufactured in the United States of America
Cover and Interior Design: Kristina Blank Makansi

Illustrations: Mark A. Montgomery
www.markamontgomery.com

In memory of my beloved parents
and forever mentors,
Mr. & Mrs. Freddie and Irene Brinson, Sr.

Glossary

Ace: A team's best starting pitcher.

Backdoor Slider: A pitch that appears to be out of the strike zone, but then breaks over the plate.

Baltimore Chop: A ground ball that hits in front of home plate and takes a large hop over the infielder's head.

Closer: Relief pitcher who specializes in pitching the last few outs of a game, generally used to hold a lead in the late innings of a game.

Cutter: A fastball with a late break in it.

Diamond: The infield playing surface.

Doubleheader: Two games played back to back by the same teams.

Fastball: A straight pitch thrown by the pitcher as hard as possible.

Hot Corner: Third Base.

Inning: A period of play. There are 9 innings in a regulation game and each team bats in an inning until they get 3 outs.

Chapter 1: The Diamond

ShaTayshia's dad and little brother were in the garden when two braids and a baseball cap whizzed by.

"Where are you running off to in such a hurry?" he asked.

"To practice."

Again?"

"Tryouts are only a week away."

"Okay, but you need to be home for dinner," he said. He picked up his gardening gloves and went into the kitchen. "Maybe I should go give her a couple of pointers."

"Um hmm," Mama cleared her throat and raised an eyebrow. "That's nice of you but remember her baseball talent comes from my side of the family."

Zing!

"Ball two," ShaTayshia chided herself. "My pitching is way off."

"If this was a game, you'd be in danger of walking the batter." ShaTayshia turned and gaped when she saw the woman sitting under a nearby shade tree. "Try that pitch again," the woman called. "But this time, arch your back, step forward, lean back again, and let it rip as you come up. That ball will sail right over the plate, but it'll be so fast, it'll be a guaranteed strike."

ShaTayshia shook her head, puzzled, but she stepped back to the mound. She didn't remember that woman sitting there when she started practicing. She thought about what the woman said and wound up.

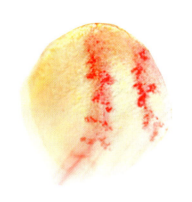

THWACK!

The ball zoomed over the plate and smacked into the fence behind the batter's box.

"Wow!" ShaTayshia shrieked, and turned toward the woman. "How did you know how to do that?"

"I know because it's how the Philadelphia Dolly Vardens played."

"Who's the Philadelphia Dolly Vardens?" Sha-Tayshia asked as she walked toward the woman.

"Who indeed? The Philadelphia Dolly Vardens was none other than the first women's professional baseball team and every single player was African American."

"What?" ShaTayshia asked, her eyes wide. "I've never heard of such a thing."

"That doesn't surprise me one bit."

"Do they still play?"

"Oh, no. This was a long time ago. During Reconstruction. You know about Reconstruction?"

"Yes. We studied it in history class."

Well, the Philadelphia Dolly Vardens got their start all the way back in the 1880s. A white businessman, probably thought he was nickel slick, thought he could make a profit by pitting two squads of all-female professional baseball players against each other in exhibition games on Sunday afternoons."

"If it was started just for that man to make money off them, why did the women play?"

"Oh, they paid no never mind to all that. You have to understand that the Dolly Vardens knew they were strong, skilled athletes. They knew the owner wanted to see them prancing around 'entertaining' the fans, but they played some real ball. They put that man in a trick bag and got the final tee hee on him."

"Just by the two squads playing each other?"

"Well, now, to fully appreciate the intensity of the competition you have to understand the amazing talent of the players. Setting it off was the starting pitcher with her 'Sweet and Sour Pitch.' Everyone called it that because it started out nice and mellow, hittable, but the batter turned sour mighty quick when the ball just passed on by and the inevitable strike was called.

"I'd love to be able to pitch like that," ShaTayshia said.

"Then there were the 'Firestorm Twins,' Jackie and Dorsey Martin. Those two were the best base stealers every." The woman chuckled and shook her head. "When they stormed a base, you just couldn't put them out. And we can't forget ShaVonne 'Blockbuster' Boggs."

"Blockbuster?"

"She'd just bust right through anybody who crowded the plate. And then there was the Hearn six—Annie Ruth, Diana, Tonya, Lena, Vanessa, and Essie. They were known for bringing the heat and shutting the other team down when they played outfield."

"Did a lot of people see them play?"

"Oh, yes. Word got around about those games and people from all over packed the stands, which meant more and more money for the owner, but not for the Dolly Vardens. And, of course, as word got out, teams were formed for white female players, too.

"Did the Dolly Vardens play the white teams?"

"No child, they never did."

"Why not?"

"Well, that was just another sign of those segregated times," The woman said with a shake of her head. Then she leaned closer to ShaTayshia and winked. "If truth be known, those white teams didn't want to feel the Dolly Varden's fire."

ShaTayshia smiled and looked at the woman.

"Do I know you? You look familiar." ShaTayshia looked at her a moment and said, "I know! You look like the woman in the photo on my auntie's mantle.

"Well, ShaTayshia I reckon' I should."

"Wait. How do you know my name?"

"I've known about you since before you were even a notion.

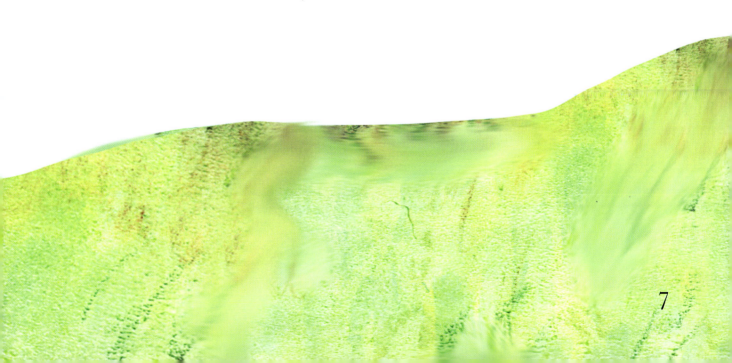

Chapter 2: The Real Deal

"Never mind that," the woman said. "I'm gonna tell you a well-kept secret, one that the owner and most other people didn't know." ShaTayshia sat up a little straighter. "Remember when I said the Dolly Vardens were serious ball players?"

ShaTayshia nodded.

"Well, I meant it. So serious that on any given Thursday after working their day jobs, the Dolly Vardens would disappear."

"Where did they go?"

"Way way out, deep deep down in a valley, on a rugged ball field. That's what most people didn't know and never did find out," she said with a chuckle.

"What were they doing?"

"They were playing doubleheaders to the rowdy cheers of our folks."

"But who'd they play?"

"Teams like the Philadelphia Pythians and the Harrisburg Monrovians."

"I've never heard of them either."

"Too bad because they were some of the best ball players ever!" The woman sighed. "A big part of our history is missing, but the Pythians and the Monrovians were two of the first African American male baseball teams."

ShaTayshia jumped up. "The Dolly Vardens played against men?"

"All the time, and I'm here to tell you those were some fiercely competitive games. Who could forget the brawl for it all, played Philly style because it was the Philadelphia Dolly Vardens against the Philadelphia Pythians. Shoot, it don't get no better than that! Now, keep in mind," the woman said, "the Pythians were already struttin' their stuff because they had just got back from Harrisburg where they beat the Monrovians 59-27."

She wrapped her arms around herself and rocked back and forth with laughter. "Whew! Now, that was a game to remember!"

"What happened?"

The woman's eyes glistened with excitement as she began. "It was the bottom of the ninth and the bases were loaded with the winning run ..."

"Batter up!"

'Knock it out to New York City!"

"Not tonight! That's the strike-out queen on the mound."

"And she's pitching to the homerun king!"

"Swing batter batter!"

"Strike two!"

"One more. Just one more! Uh-oh. See how he's shaking and shuddering? That's becauser her pitches have a wiggle the worms wanna learn."

"What you talkin'?"

"You'll see. Her next pitch is gonna wiggle right past his bat and he'll be outta there! Ha! Another Ace strikeout! And the Philadelphia Pythians are still in trouble because ShaVonne "Blockbuster' Boggs is the first batter!"

"Time for dinner!" ShaTayshia's mom's voice rang out from across the ball field "Come on in."

"Just a minute!" ShaTayshia replied. "I'm listening to—" She looked around, but she was all alone.

Chapter 3: In Justice

Whew! ShaTayshia had played the whole time in both games. She'd made every one of her plays and had even hit a home run. Tryouts were tough, but her hard work and practice had paid off.

The whistle blew and coach nodded toward the dugout. "Good job, people. If you made the first cut, your name will be on the posted list."

Everyone ran to the dugout and crowded around the list. And then tears of frustration filled ShaTayshia's eyes and she stormed off. Twenty minutes later, she was kicking the dirt and throwing her glove in the tree by the neighborhood ball diamond.

"It's so unfair!" She kicked the dirt again.

"Are you done?"

Huffing and puffing from all her anger, ShaTayshia whirled around to see the strangely familiar woman again.

"Good. Now climb up there and get your glove."

ShaTayshia hoisted herself up branch by branch until she could grab her glove from where it was wedged. Then she threw it down and dropped to the ground after it.

"Now," the woman said, patting the bench beside her, "come on over here and sit down. Tell me what you're going on about."

"I can't make the team no matter how hard I try."

"Can't, huh?"

Braids swinging forward, head down, ShaTayshia muttered, "No, I can't.

"Is that what you really think?"

ShaTayshia nodded.

"Well then, the first thing you need to do is put can't in a can and Baltimore Chop it."

"What?"

"Baltimore Chop that can't," the woman repeated. "I know you can because I just saw you wearing those players out with some of the best pitching I've ever witnessed. Especially your backdoor slider when the other team's faster player was riding the hot corner."

"If that's true, then why didn't I make the team? It's not fair."

"Tsk, tsk. You seem to think things won't go wrong sometimes just because you're trying to do everything right. No doubt about it, you were the ace in the first game."

"Really?"

"Girl? Yes! Why do you think they made you the closer in the second one? You struck out three players in a row. You were on fire! And I know a thing or two about great pitchers, if I say so myself. But, I also know that things don't always go as planned."

"What are you supposed to do when things aren't fair?"

"You really like waving around that 'fair' banner don't you?" The woman leaned forward. "Let me give you some shock and awe information about fair. Now, you take the Pythians. They applied for membership with the National Association of Baseball Players just a few months after the Philadelphia Dolly Vardens became a team. But they were denied entry with a crafty little rule that stated no team with one or more African American players could be admitted. Is that fair?"

"No, ma'am."

"And let me tell you about Joseph B. Pole, one of the best players the Monrovians had. Before Emancipation, there was a standoff between some Virginia slaveholders and a crowd of Harrisburg black folk, and our Joseph managed to pry open a locked door to help a slave escape and then got a vicious beating for protesting unfair treatment. Was that fair?"

"No! That's not fair at all!"

"Now, did I tell you how the Philadelphia Dolly Vardens got their name?"

"Because they lived in Philadelphia?"

"There's more to the story than that. You see, Dolly Varden was the name of a type of dress. It had a tight bodice and bouffant bloomers over a calf-length petticoat and men liked to see women in it. Men liked it so much that people started calling ladies who wore the style Dolly Vardens. The original name came from a Charles Dickens character. You ever read Charles Dickens?"

ShaTayshia shook her head.

"Just like there's always time for baseball, there's always time for reading," the woman said.

ShaTayshia nodded in agreement. "I know, reading is one of my favorite things to do."

"Well, the owner knew that with a name like Dolly Vardens, the men would come see the games. The players even had to wear red calico dresses and play with a big ol' ball of red yarn. So those ladies had to play in dresses, not uniforms like the men wore. And they played with a ball of yarn, not a real baseball. Think that's fair?"

"Not at all."

"And the owner raked in the profits which he kept for himself. He hardly paid those ladies at all. But that's okay."

"Okay? How could that be okay?" ShaTayshia asked.

The woman leaned back and looked out at the baseball field. "You see, down in that valley where they played on their own field of dreams, they were champions. Throwing a baseball 95 miles an hour ain't easy, but not only was the ace pitcher for the Dolly Vardens one of the best at it, but she had to do it with that ball of yarn. And besides, those red calico costumes served a purpose, too.

"How?"

"That material was real sturdy, which was a good thing because the players wore them twice a week. And that bright red sure did come in handy when sliding into home plate because the umpire couldn't miss the player even when all that dust was swirling around."

ShaTayshia laughed. "For real?"

"You know it. And there's one more thing to remember."

"Yes?"

"All kinds of unfair things can happen, so to make it through life, there are some things you have to do on a regular basis."

"Like what?"

"You have to step up. If you trip or get shoved headfirst, you gotta shake it off and step up. Even when things seem so unfair you feel like you're trapped in cement, you just shake it off and step up."

"Shake it off and step up." ShaTayshia repeated.

"Now, you say you didn't make the team. What are you gonna do?"

"Shake it off and step up."

"That's right. You love baseball and want to play on a team, you have to—"

"Shake it off and step up," they declared in unison.

Chapter 4: Trying Times

"Hey Sis, whatcha doing?" Lil' Freddie asked his big sister.

ShaTayshia smiled down at him and peered through the fence behind home plate. "Right now, I'm trying to hit a homerun. After that, I'm gonna practice my pitching."

"You trying out for the team again?"

"Yup." She tossed the ball in the air and pounded it toward left field. "And when I make it, I'm going to teach you the secret of the Sweet and Sour pitch."

"Now, you're talking."

ShaTayshia turned to see the woman settle into the bench under the nearby tree. She picked up her glove and trotted over to her.

"I knew you'd be out here practicing, out here stepping up. You've got baseball in your blood, you know," the woman said with a smile.

"I'm ready," ShaTayshia proclaimed, double tapping her glove.

The woman raised her eyebrows. "Is that a new glove?"

"No. It's my same old glove, but the red laces are new."

"Well, that's a mighty fine look, indeed," the woman smiled.

"It's in honor of the Philadelphia Dolly Vardens. I know now I have to shake it off and step up. Can't is in a can, and there are three more teams holding tryouts next month. I'm going to be ready!"

The woman nodded. "And if—"

"And if it turns out to be cement," ShaTayshia chimed in, "I'll just have to blast out of it, even if it takes another year of practice."

"I know you will. Forever and a day, I expect nothing less. But now, I've got to go." The woman stood and turned to leave.

"Wait! You never told me your name. I looked at the photo on my auntie's mantle and it's a picture of my—"

"You already know my name, honey." The woman tapped ShaTayshia's glove. "And now that we've met, you know a whole lot more besides." She winked and tapped the glove again.

ShaTayshia looked down at her glove and slowly opened it. She looked up in amazement, but the woman was gone. Poof! One moment she was there and the next, nothing.

"No." ShaTayshia shook her head and laughed. "It's impossible! It just can't be." She picked up the big ol' ball of red yarn nestled inside her glove and then took off running toward her little brother. She couldn't wait to tell him that Irene Hunter, their great, great, great, great grandmother, a freed slave, threw the first fast ball as The Ace, the left-handed pitcher for the Philadelphia Dolly Vardens, the first women's professional baseball team ever.

Did You Know?

While reading the book did you guess that there was a relationship between ShaTayshia and the mysterious woman before it was revealed at the end of the story? If so, how did you know? Ready for some new discoveries? Now that you know ShaTayshia's great, great, great, great grandmother was the ace pitcher for the Philadelphia Dolly Vardens, rereading the book can be even more fun and more meaningful when you spot clues to their connection. What is special about the shirt the mysterious woman is wearing? How about the ball ShaTayshia is tossing in her glove? What is the tip off that both ShaTayshia and the mysterious woman are baseball players? How does ShaTayshia finally discover the identity of the mysterious woman? What other connections can you discover?

About the Author

Dr. Sabrina A. Brinson is an African American scholar and a diversity consultant. Her educational background includes an AA in General Studies, a BA in Psychology, a BA in English Literature, a MA in Special Education, with an emphasis in Behavior Disorders, and a PhD in Curriculum and Instruction, with an emphasis in Early Childhood Education, and a cognate in Reading. Her passion and advocacy for reading is reflected in the national, community-based, literacy programs she founded and directs, "Boys Booked on Barbershops and Girls Booked on Beautyshops." Reading nooks with a variety of culturally sustaining children's books are set up in barbershops and beautyshops across the nation. Picture it! Children reading or being read to while waiting to get into barber and beautician chairs.

Dr. Brinson is also a community activist striving for equity and inclusion for all, a full professor at a Midwestern university, and a native of Tampa, Florida.

Meet the Philadelphia Dolly Vardens, is the first book in a series entitled, "Strength beyond Measure." The series is designed as curricula to enhance children's overall development (e.g., cognitive, social, and emotional) with resulting benefits of strong self-worth, information, inspiration, and pleasure. Primary objectives of the series are to bridge historical omissions; feature notable achievements of both known and little known individuals from diverse populations; highlight the proactive ingenuity and resilience utilized to overcome obstacles; and, actively engage readers in the books with opportunities to think critically, form predictions, and make intriguing discoveries about the main characters through clues along the way. As a result, *Meet the Philadelphia Dolly Vardens*, was written to heighten awareness about the first American women's professional baseball team. It was also important to show the effectiveness of positive action steps in the face of unfair practices, and the importance of hard work and perseverance to achieve goals. Overall, caps off for the timeless reverberating message demonstrated by both the Philadelphia Dolly Vardens and ShaTayshia, "Strong has always been the real pretty."

About the Illustrator

Mark is an old soul from the suburbs of Kansas City. Some of his greatest inspirations are bits of Americana: Jazz, Blues, Bluegrass, Old Movies, Barbeque and the Dust Bowl Era of the 1930s. His artistic heroes include Pablo Picasso, Henri de Toulouse-Lautrec, Al Hirschfeld, Thomas Hart Benton, Stanton MacDonald-Wright, Diego Rivera and Miguel Covarrubias. He loves vintage texture and explores color, shape and movement from Cubism, Futurism and Synchronism. He is a BIG fan of illustration. He still works and lives in the Midwest with his family. On his birthday, he eats dry ribs and takes the family to a movie.

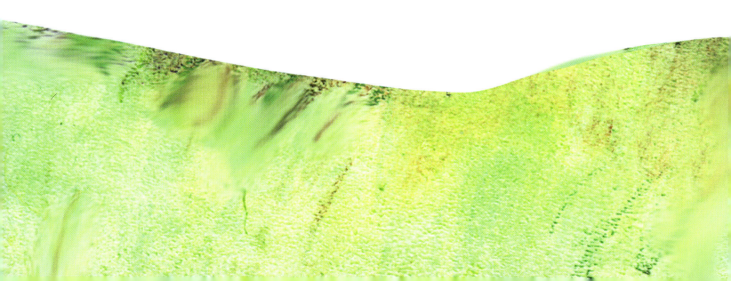